10-7 FOR GOOD SAM

10-7 FOR GOOD SAM

By Bob Cunningham

Illustrations by Rod and Barbara Furan

Library of Congress Catalog Card Number: 76-051143. International Standard Book Number: 0-913940-59-3.

It was early morning rush-hour time in Cascade City.

The freeways and feeder roads were jammed with cars and trucks. There were buses and motorcycles and cement mixers and garbage mashers. There were huge double bottoms from California and Seattle, heading for downtown truck terminals. Delivery vans carried bread and milk, newspapers and TV parts. Big 18-wheelers crawled toward the city with loads of food and machines and goods for stores to sell.

Neil Hawkins guided his station wagon into the stream of traffic from a ramp.

"Traffic flowing pretty good for a Monday," he said to the man sitting beside him. "Let's read the mail a little and see how it's looking further in." He switched on the CB radio mounted beneath the dash.

A tangle of voices burst out of the speaker.

"Breaker for a southbounder out of Seattle on this here Big Nickel."

"Anybody got a 10-13 on Route 26 over the mountain?"

"Mercy sakes, some turkey's got a busted skin right in the Harrison off-ramp. You good buddies want to use Franklin as an alternate. Good Sam, KEK-0012, 10-10 and watchin'."

TO THE READER: ALL CB TERMS ARE EXPLAINED IN THE GLOSSARY ON PAGES 30-31.

"How 'bout it, Chicken Guts, you got a copy?"

"Breaker for some local information —"

"Breaker for a Smokey report —"

"Fat chance, dude! Only way you hammer down on this six-lane parking lot is if you sprout wings and fly!"

"Ten-fo' on the cookin' slow!"

"Breaker One-Seven for a 10-36."

"Eight-eleven."

"We got a real slow-down on the Iron Bridge, westbounders. If you can find a good alternative, use it. Good Sam, KEK-0012, clear and on the job."

Neil said: "That's good to know. We won't take that bridge on the way to the newspaper office."

Neil was the outdoor editor of the Cascade City Journal. He wrote stories about fishing, hunting, camping, outdoor subjects and his favorite hobby, CB radio.

This morning, Neil had picked up his brother, Denny, at the airport. Denny had business in the Pacific Northwest and had stopped in to see Neil as well.

"How come I can't understand what these guys on the radio are saying?" Denny asked.

Neil laughed. "CB radio has a language all its own. If you just listen in — that's what I meant by 'reading the mail' — you catch on quickly."

As the voices continued to crackle out of the speaker, Neil translated for his brother. A 10-36 was a request for the correct time. A 10-13 was a request for road and weather conditions. A Smokey Bear was a policeman, especially a state trooper who wore a wide-brimmed hat. A good buddy was anyone who talked over CB radio. A ratchet-jaw was somebody who talked too much.

"What about a Good Sam?" Denny asked. The station wagon went through an interchange and crossed the wide Cascade River that split the city in half.

"See those hills to the west?"

Denny nodded. Houses clung to the green slopes that overlooked downtown Cascade City.

"Somewhere up there lives the commuter's best friend. His handle is Good Sam, short for Good Samaritan. He has strong binoculars, a CB radio, and a perfect view of all of the main freeways and bridges feeding into the city. Every morning and evening, at rush-hour time, Sam is on the job. He looks for traffic tie-ups. Things like blocked lanes, stalled cars, roadwork, bottleneck jams. Sam tells us about them over the radio. Then we can try to avoid the bad spots."

"Who is this Good Sam?" asked Denny.

"Nobody knows," Neil said. "Except maybe the FCC. That's the Federal Communications Commission, the part of the government that deals with radio operations. They have a listing of all call letters."

"Some of those guys we listened to didn't use call letters."

"That's illegal," Neil said. "Guys who do that are asking for a bust."

The car turned into the newspaper parking garage then, and the brothers forgot about CB radio. After Neil took his brother on a tour of the plant, Denny went off to take care of his own business.

Late in the afternoon, the brothers met again. They drove onto the freeway and headed for Neil's home, some 20 miles south of the city.

The superhighway was clogged with vehicles that barely crawled along. "Better ask Good Sam what the big hold-up is," Neil said. He switched on his radio and keyed the mike. "How about it, Good Sam? What's keepin' us from boogying on this southbound boulevard? Come on back to Sky Hawk, KCW-0484."

He released the mike button. A voice came back. "Haven't heard a squeak from Sam tonight. This jam is at least two miles long, wonder what's causing it. KGEO-3452, the Saddle Tramp, is by."

Neil shook his head in puzzlement. "Sam's been faithful for nearly two years. Something must really be wrong if he's 10-7 during the rush-hour."

"What's 10-7?" asked Denny.

"Off the air." Neil got onto the radio again and asked if anyone else had heard Sam, but he always got the same reply:

"Negatory, good buddy. Far as I know, Sam is 10-7 tonight, just when we need him bad!"

They were stuck in traffic nearly an hour. The delay was caused by a wreck two miles out of town. The next morning, when Neil drove Denny back to the airport, there was still no word from the helpful CB traffic reporter.

STATE
POLICE

It was the same during the rest of the week. Good Sam had vanished from the airwaves. The trucking channel was abuzz with CB mobiles wondering what had happened to their friend. He was badly missed.

On Friday, Neil sat at his typewriter and wrote a special article. When the afternoon edition of the Journal hit the stands, there was a long piece with the byline of Neil Hawkins. It had a photo of a big traffic jam and a wistful headline:

GOOD SAM, WHY ARE YOU 10-7?

The story about Good Sam got results right away. Early the next morning, Neil's phone rang. It was the city editor of the newspaper.

"We've got a follow-up on your Good Sam piece," he said. "Get on out to 267 Hilltop Road. A Mrs. Mary Gilbert. Take Sara for the photos, if any."

I'm on my way," said Neil. His wife, Sara, was a free-lance photographer. Usually she takes photos of wildlife and beautiful scenery. On this morning, she would use her camera on a very different subject.

The Hawkins' drove to a shabby little house high in the hills west of Cascade City. When they rang the bell, a careworn, gray-haired woman invited them to come in.

"I read your story in the paper," Mrs. Gilbert told them. "I thought maybe you could help." She turned and called out: "Larry! Will you come here?"

There was a pause. Then Sara and Neil heard a faint squeaking sound. A wheelchair came rolling into the tiny living room of the Gilbert home. In it was a teenage boy with a shy smile.

Neil knew who it was. He stuck out his hand in greeting. "Howdy-do, Good Sam! I'm Sky Hawk, and this is my XYL, Pigeon Hawk. Sorry you've gone 10-7. We're here to see if we can do something about that!"

Larry's story was very sad. A rare disease had left him unable to walk and too weak for regular school classes. A teacher visited him at home twice a week. Sometimes he went on outings with other handicapped young people. But for most of the time, Larry Gilbert stayed home with his widowed mother.

He traveled by means of his CB radio.

Neil looked at the old set, now silent. He admired Good Sam's powerful binoculars, which had belonged to his late father. "He was first mate on a freighter," Larry said proudly. "No matter how bad things get for us, I'll never give up these glasses."

"I think things will get better soon," Neil said. "I'd like to tell your story in the newspaper. There are a lot of people who miss your rush-hour traffic reports."

"I like to be helpful," Good Sam said. "It makes me feel like I'm good for something after all."

"Nobody is ever useless," Sara insisted.

"I used to think I was," Good Sam said softly, until Mom got me this old second hand CB radio. The antenna is a piece of junk, but it was all we could afford. The radio's broken down on me before, and I was always able to fix it. But this time —"

He shrugged his narrow shoulders.

"We'll get you 10-8 again," Neil said. "Soon."

Neil interviewed both Larry and his mother. Sara took pictures of Good Sam, studying the freeways with his binoculars, microphone in hand.

The article that Neil wrote when he got home would not appear in the paper until Monday. "I'm not going to wait that long," Neil declared. "We're going to get the ball rolling for Good Sam this very weekend."

"What are you going to do, Neil?" asked Sara.

"Something that other CBers in other parts of the country have done. We're going to have a marathon for Good Sam!"

Neil, Sara, and their son Ryan and daughter Kristi set up the marathon to run from Saturday night until Sunday night. "We'll take turns, and we'll try to hit each channel every ten minutes with the story. Remember, FCC rules limit each transmission to five minutes. We should need less than half that time to tell Good Sam's story. We'll ask everyone who replies to send a donation to the Good Sam Fund, care of the Journal."

"It sounds like a wonderful idea, Dad," said Kristi. "How can it miss?"

They were going to find out very soon.

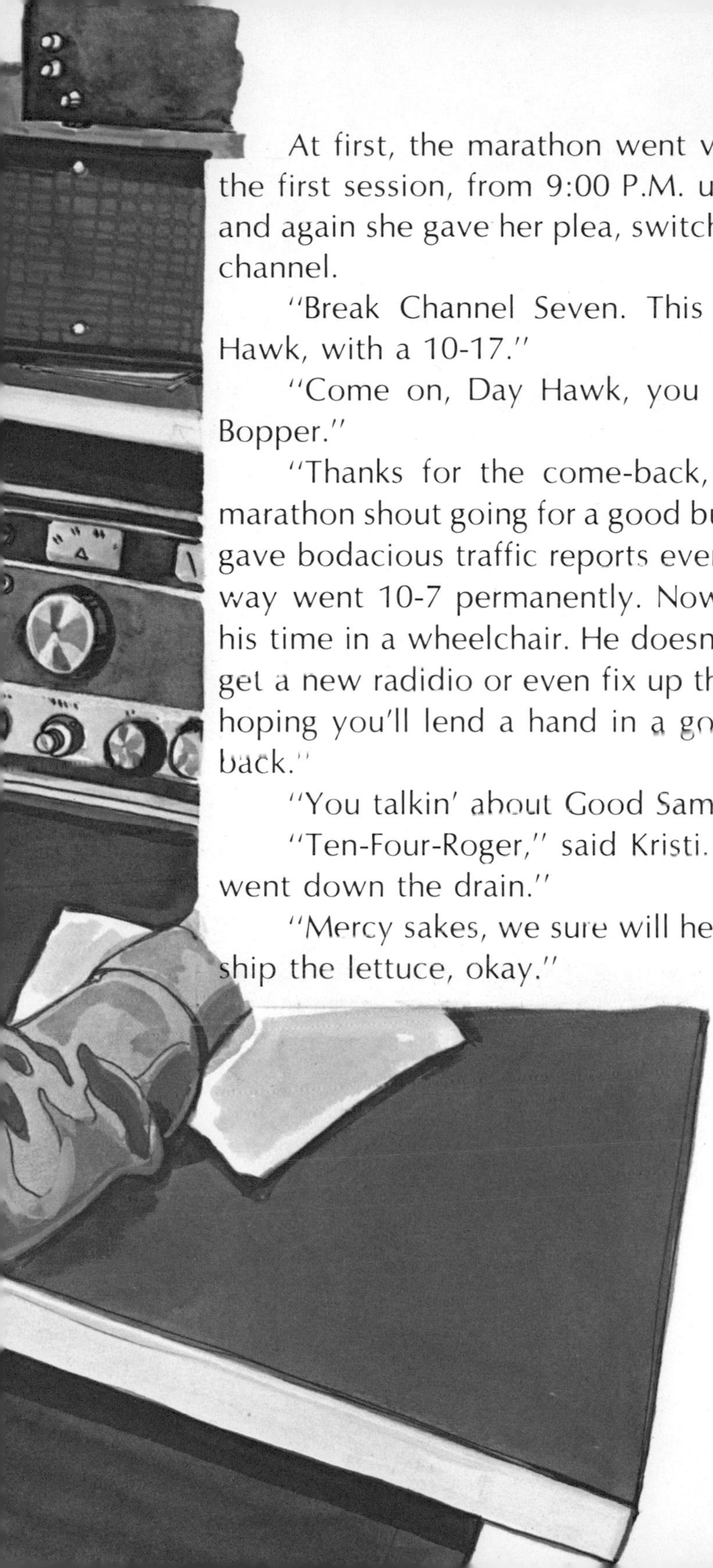

At first, the marathon went very well. Kristi took the first session, from 9:00 P.M. until midnight. Again and again she gave her plea, switching from channel to channel.

"Break Channel Seven. This is KCW-0484, Day Hawk, with a 10-17."

"Come on, Day Hawk, you got the Bean-Town Bopper."

"Thanks for the come-back, Bopper. We got a marathon shout going for a good buddy hereabouts. He gave bodacious traffic reports every day until his two-way went 10-7 permanently. Now, this rascal spends his time in a wheelchair. He doesn't have the bread to get a new radidio or even fix up the old one. So we're hoping you'll lend a hand in a good cause. Come on back."

"You talkin' about Good Sam?"

"Ten-Four-Roger," said Kristi. "His ole modulator went down the drain."

"Mercy sakes, we sure will help. Just tell where to ship the lettuce, okay."

Kristi spelled out the newspaper's address, thanked the CBer, and switched to the next channel. Everything seemed to go perfectly until just after 11 o'clock. She made her call on Channel 13 and a very powerful station answered her.

"This here's the Mad-Mad-Mad Madball comin' back at ya, Day Hawk Dolly. I wanta know just how long you gonna bucket-mouth it all over this here air, c'mon."

"We're doing the marathon for a good cause. We don't talk for more than a few minutes on any channel. Will you help us?"

"Oh, nega-tine, li'l beaver. Like, who cares if some loser is 10-7? Who cares if a flock of turkeys get stuck in traffic? That's their tough luck for havin' to go to work!"

A loud crackle of laughter came over the air. It was followed by duck quacks and a weird noise like a siren. "You read? You dig? Now you quit hoggin' the air and let the big time modulators holler in peace. The Mad-Mad-Mad Madball is talkin'!"

Kristi said angrily, "KCW-0484 is 10-27 to One-Four."

She switched to Channel 14. Madball was waiting. "Now, I didn't say switch, little Day Hawk Dolly. I said quit!" Another chorus of quacks and howls rang out.

Kristi said slowly, "Those noises you're transmitting are a big 10-30. If you interfere with my transmission, that violates FCC rules, too."

"Aha! Aha!" crowed Madball. "You are the one buckin' for a visit from the candy man, li'l fox. Askin' for money over the air is a big no-no. What d'you think of that? Quack-quack-quack weeeeoo!

Neil came into the radio shack and said: "About time for me to take over, Kristi."

"That's a big Ten-Four," she said.

Neil picked up the mike and keyed it. "KCW-0484, Sky Hawk here. What's your problem, Sonny?"

"Sonny? Sonny?" Madball was clearly enraged at being thought a little boy. He quacked wildly and used his illegal oscillator, which made a howling noise when it was keyed near a microphone.

Neil merely switched to Channel 15 and gave a call. He reached his old friend Mountain Goat and began to tell him about Good Sam.

"Hey, Neil, you're breaking up bad. Somebody's throwing a carrier on you I —"

Goat's voice cut off. There was a hissing sound. Then came Madball's laugh, a quack and a howl.

Neil waited for a moment. Then he tried to talk again. But Mountain Goat said: "That clown is still mashin' the mike on you. Go land-line. KGU-1756 down."

Neil went to the telephone and put in a quick call to his friend. It's a crazy one, Mountain Goat. He was doing a 10-75 all over Kristi. Probably the sick way he gets his laughs. Sounds like a young kid with an expensive new toy."

"To bad he didn't bother to read the rules that come with it," said Goat. "Spoilers like that deserve a blanket party. You get back on the air with him, Neil. I'll set up a 10-1000."

"Yeah, Ten-Four. I guess it's the only way."

Neil hung up and went back to the radio. He switched to Channel 20 and got most of his marathon message across before Madball tracked him down.

The annoying quacks, howls, and smothering carrier waves kept interfering with Neil's transmissions for over an hour.

Sara was very worried. "If he keeps it up all night, the marathon will be spoiled. She wondered, was he right about it being illegal to ask for money over the air?"

"It's illegal," Neil said, "only if you keep money for yourself. Charitable marathons like ours are perfectly legal. Don't worry. This boy is going to get his quacker cooled any minute now."

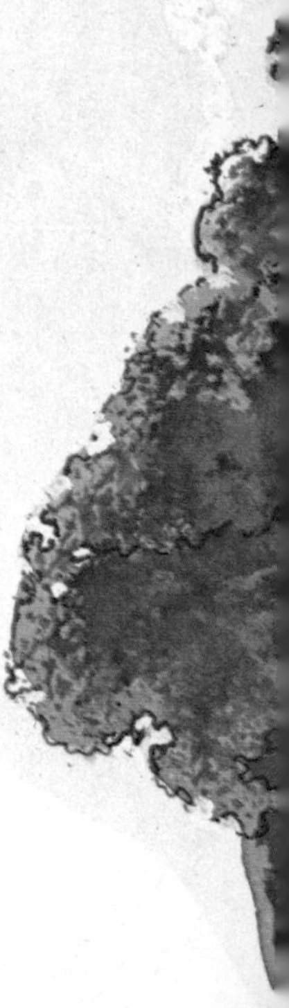

Some two miles away, an FCC van prowled the dark streets of a Cascade City suburb. The houses were handsome and expensive. Many of them had CB antennas on the roof. The van cruised up one street and down the next. Sometimes it slowed . . . as though it were listening.

It rolled up in front of a large house and stopped. For a full fifteen minutes, it sat there, yellow parking lights glowing like animal eyes. Then two men got out of the van, walked to the front door of the house, and rang the bell.

Two minutes later, Madball went off the air. Forever.

A week passed, then one evening, a caravan of cars that sprouted antennas came rolling up to Good Sam's place. Larry's mother rolled her surprised son out onto the stoop as the CBers clapped and cheered.

Neil stepped forward. "On behalf of all the friendly modulators of Cascade City, I present you with this check for $3,286.42! It represents the results of a CB marathon, plus gifts sent in by Journal readers to the Good Sam Fund."

Applause, whistles, and shouts followed!

"There's more!" Neil said. "The money can be used for a scholarship — maybe to radio school. To give Good Sam ears again, we have a really great gift from Mr. Al Jones of AJ Electronics!"

A smiling man stepped forward with a carton. Eyes sparkling with tears, Good Sam received a splendid new base-station radio.

"To be sure that everybody reads those Good Sam reports 10-2 —" Neil pointed to two men, who were unloading a batch of pipes and wires from an unmarked van. "We also have, courtesy of Uncle Charley, a beautiful new $400 antenna! Slightly used."

"The parents of the previous owner said that he wouldn't be needing it any more," remarked one of the FCC men. "So we suggested that Good Sam would give it a good home."

"Roger-Four for sure!" said Good Sam. "Thanks a million good buddies. I'll be 10-10 and standing by."

A.J.
ELECTRONICS
'CB'
UP
FRAGILE

CB GLOSSARY

BEAVER — pretty girl or woman
BIG NICKEL — Interstate 5
BLANKET PARTY — operation that silences pesty CB operator
BODACIOUS — excellent
BOOGY — travel in vehicle; go someplace
BOULEVARD — freeway or superhighway
BREAKER — (1) request for channel use; (2) person who wants to transmit
BREAKING UP — signal not received clearly
BUCKET-MOUTH — CBer who talks too much or hogs channel; also ratchet-jaw
BUST — arrest; citation by FCC for illegal use of radio
BUSTED SKIN — flat tire; also PUNKIN
BY — standing by; waiting for contact
CALL LETTERS — letter-number combination assigned to radio operator as part of FCC license to transmit
CANDY MAN — FCC inspector who polices CB operations
CB — Citizens Band radio
CHANNEL — frequency assigned for CB use
CLEAR — finished transmitting
COME ON BACK — reply to my transmission
COOKING — traveling in vehicle
COPY — (1) message; (2) to hear or listen in
DOUBLE BOTTOM — a semi truck hauling two trailers
DOWN THE DRAIN — (1) broken; (2) not heard, as a transmission
EARS — a CB radio
EIGHTEEN WHEELER — semi-trailer truck
FCC — Federal Communications Commission, government agency that regulates and polices all radio operations; also UNCLE CHARLEY, CANDY MAN, FEDS; 10-1000
FOX — pretty girl or woman
GOOD BUDDY — common name for CB operator
HAMMER DOWN — accelerate vehicle; speed
HOLLER — call for person over CB radio; also SHOUT
HOW ABOUT IT — call for a certain CB station; invitation to transmit
LETTUCE — money
MARATHON — lengthy CB operation, usually to raise money for charity
MASHING THE MIKE — transmitting dead carrier to blot out another station's message, an illegal action; also known as THROWING CARRIER

MODULATOR — (1) a CB operator; (2) a CB radio
NEGATINE — negative response; no
NEGATORY — negative response; no
ONE-SEVEN — Channel 17, used by truckers in parts of Pacific Northwest; other trucker channels include 19, 10, 12, and others, depending upon section of country
RADIDIO — CB radio (pronounced ruh-DID-ee-oh)
RASCAL — name for CB operator, especially trucker
RATCHET-JAW — CBer who talks too much or hogs channel; also BUCKET-MOUTH
READ THE MAIL — listen to other CB transmissions
ROGER-FOUR — yes; also TEN-FOUR, FOUR-ROGER, etc.
SHOUT — call for person over CB radio; also HOLLER
SIX-LANE PARKING LOT — superhighway with slow moving traffic
SMOKEY BEAR — police officer; also SMOKEY
SMOKEY REPORT — information about police vehicle positions and speed traps
SOUTHBOUNDER — vehicle southbound on highway
STAND BY — wait for message or call
10-2 — receiving well
10-4 — affirmative; yes; okay; message received
10-7 — off the air
10-8 — on the air
10-10 — standing by
10-13 — request weather and road condition
10-17 — important message
10-27 — move to Channel
10-30 — violation of FCC rules
10-36 — request correct time
10-75 — you are causing interference
10-1000 — FCC inspector
TEN-FO' — affirmative; yes
TEN-FOUR-ROGER — emphatic yes
THROW A CARRIER — blot out another's transmission by broadcasting unmodulated signal; also MASHING THE MIKE
TURKEY — a silly or luckless person
TWO-WAY — a CB radio
UNCLE CHARLEY — FCC inspector
WESTBOUNDER — vehicle westbound on highway
XYL — wife; literally, "ex-Young Lady," a ham radio term adopted by CBers; YL is girl friend; XYD is daughter